TALK ABOUT THE MONSTER

Written by
Mistofer Christopher

Illustrated by
Mike Hogan

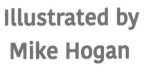

From the House of Mistofer Christopher

For all the children and children at heart
For all that fight fear…

o my Mom, Dad, and Granny who gave their best and their all for their family.
To my twin sister, Juliana, who was my first womb mate and soul friend.
To my best friend, Mark, who told me as a teenager,
"Talk about the monster, bro." To Joselyn Clark and Michael Hogan
and all the beautiful people who have encouraged me along the way.

A book from the House of Mistofer Christopher | www.mistoferchristopher.com
Printed by Ingram
Text Copyright @2016 Mistofer Christopher
Illustration copyright @2018 Mistofer Christopher
Graphic Layout - Josie Lynn | www. JosieLynnBooks.com

Publisher's Cataloging-in-Publication data
Names: Miller, Christopher J., author. | Hogan, Michael P., illustrator.
Title: Talk about the monster / written by Mistofer Christopher ; illustrated by Michael Hogan.
Description: Queens, NY: House of Mistofer Christopher, 2018.
Identifiers: ISBN 978-1-7321266-1-9 | LCCN 2018948056
Summary: A girl faces a monster, understands it, and conquers her fear.
Subjects: LCSH Monsters--Juvenile fiction. | Girls--Juvenile fiction. | Fear--Juvenile fiction. |
BISAC JUVENILE FICTION /Monsters | JUVENILE FICTION / Social Themes / Emotions & Feelings
Classification: LCC PZ7.M61256 Tal 2018 | DDC [E]--dc23

Welcome to the House of Mistofer Christopher
Follow us: Instagram: Mistofer_Christopher | Facebook: Mistofer Christopher

Printed in the United States of America

When you talk about the Monster
you bring him down to size.
The first thing you do is start with his eyes.
Were they square? Were they round?
Was he looking at the ground?

Were they beady with a wrinkle and made you want to tinkle? When you talk about the Monster you bring him down to size.

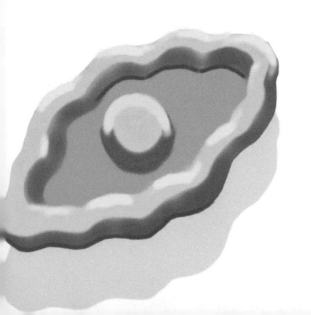

Next thing to do is you look at his ears.
It will help you to quell your ugly, bugly fears.
Was it one? Was it three? Or was it only two?
Was it eight, seven, six? Did they make you go

wheeeew?

Were they large and kinda floppy?
Or were they pointy, sorta sloppy?
When you talk about the Monster
you bring him down to size.

So tell me 'bout his nose

Was it a button or a hose?

Was it long and sorta sticky?

Or was it short and really icky?

Did he **sniffle** and kinda **Snortle?**

Or did he **snuffle** and sorta **chortle?**

When you talk about the Monster
you bring him down to size.

Let's not forget about his teeth. How many did you see?

Was it one and one and two? Or was it only three?

Were they crooked? Were they clean?
Were they hidden? Were they mean?

Floss

Were they cotton? Were they rocks?
Or were they smelly, welly socks?
When you talk about the Monster
you bring him down to size.

Did he have a lot to say?

Did you ask him 'bout his day?

Was he early? Was he late?

Did he break his breakfast plate?

Did he have his cup of Joe?

Did he drop it on his toe?

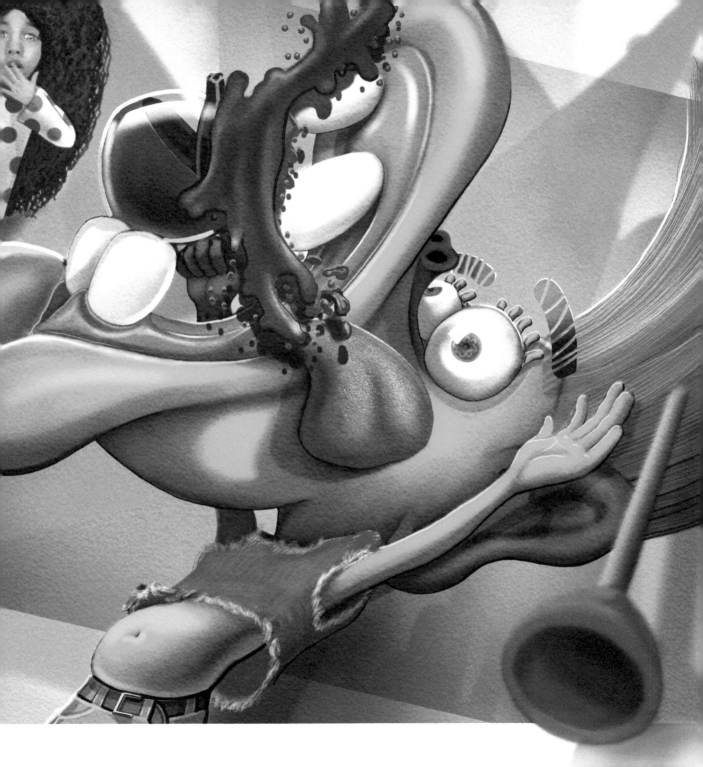

When you talk about the Monster
you bring him down to size.

Look at his clothes. What did he wear?

Was it tight? Was it loose? Or was he only hair?

Was he neat and clean and tidy?

Or did he have a lotta spidies?

Was he strong or was he jelly?
Or was he short and had a belly?
When you talk about the Monster
you bring him down to size.

Did he cough with a rattle?

Or did he giggle with a cackle?

Was his voice hoarse and raspy?

Or was it gruff and kinda nasty

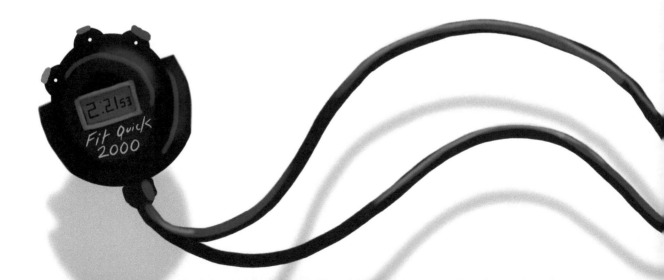

with a snivel and a dribble
while he looked for a little nibble?
When you talk about the Monster
You bring him down to size.

So surely you can see
your fear don't gotta be
'cause you have the monster key
and he's waiting by the door
drinking monster tea.

So whatcha gonna do
'cause it's really up to you?
He's trying to say goodbyes...
So you...

Talk about the Monster

and bring him down to size.

CPSIA information can be obtained
at www.ICGtesting.com
Printed in the USA
BVHW021237040219
539399BV00010B/110/P